PIGGLES' GUIDE TO...

SPACE SHUTTLES

BY KIRSTY HOLMES

WINDMILL
BOOKS ™

Published in 2019 by **Windmill Books**,
an imprint of Rosen Publishing
29 East 21st Street, New York, NY 10010

Written by: Kristy Holmes
Edited by: Holly Duhig
Designed by: Danielle Rippengill

Cataloging-in-Publication Data

Names: Holmes, Kirsty.
Title: Piggles' guide to space shuttles / Kirsty Holmes.
Description: New York : Windmill Books, 2019.
| Series: Pigs might fly! | Includes glossary and index.
Identifiers: ISBN 9781538390986 (pbk.) | ISBN
9781508197430 (library bound) | ISBN 9781538390993
(6 pack)Subjects: LCSH: Space shuttles--Juvenile literature.
Classification: LCC TL795.515 H645 2019
| DDC 629.47'4--dc23

Printed in the United States of America

CPSIA compliance information: Batch # BW19WM:
For Further Information contact Rosen Publishing,
New York, New York at 1-800-237-9932

IMAGE CREDITS

All images are courtesy of Shutterstock.com, unless otherwise specified. With thanks to Getty Images, Thinkstock Photo and iStockphoto.
Cover – NotionPic, A–R–T, logika600, BiterBig, Malchev, Alongkorn Sanguansook. 1 – BiterBig. 2 – Suiraton, Nadya_Art, NotionPic,
Alongkorn Sanguansook. 3 – BiterBig. 4 – Mascha Tace, Stock_VectorSale. 5 – Mascha Tace. NotionPic. 6 – Nadya_Art, Dzianis_Rakhuba.
7 – Macrovector, NotionPic, Alongkorn Sanguansook. 8 & 9 – Nadya_Art, NotionPic, Alongkorn Sanguansook, BiterBig. 10 – YUCALORA.
11 – Top Vector Studio, Graphic.mooi, NotionPic, Alongkorn Sanguansook. 12 & 13 – Nadya_Art, Dzianis_Rakhuba. 13 – 4zevar, iconer, BiterBig.
14 – Pogorelova Olga, Nadya_Art. 15 – Suiraton, Nadya_Art, NotionPic, Alongkorn Sanguansook. 16 – Suiraton, Teguh Jati Prasetyo, NotionPic,
Alongkorn Sanguansook. 17 – NotionPic, Alongkorn Sanguansook, Graphiqa Stock, Julia's Art. 18 – Nadya_Art, Dzianis_Rakhuba, bhjary.
19 – Igrapop, Andrey Vyrypaev. 20 – Mascha Tace, NotionPic, BiterBig. 21 – BiterBig, NotionPic, ArtMalivanov, DRogatnev. 22 – Michael Beetlov,
lukpedclub, BiterBig. 23 – Suiraton, Nadya_Art, NotionPic, Alongkorn Sanguansook. 24 – BiterBig.

CONTENTS

WORDS THAT LOOK LIKE <u>this</u> CAN BE FOUND IN THE GLOSSARY ON PAGE 24.

WELCOME TO FLIGHT SCHOOL!

So you're interested in space shuttles? Do you dream of zooming through the stars in a giant rocket? Then you've come to the right place! The Sty in the Sky Flight School!

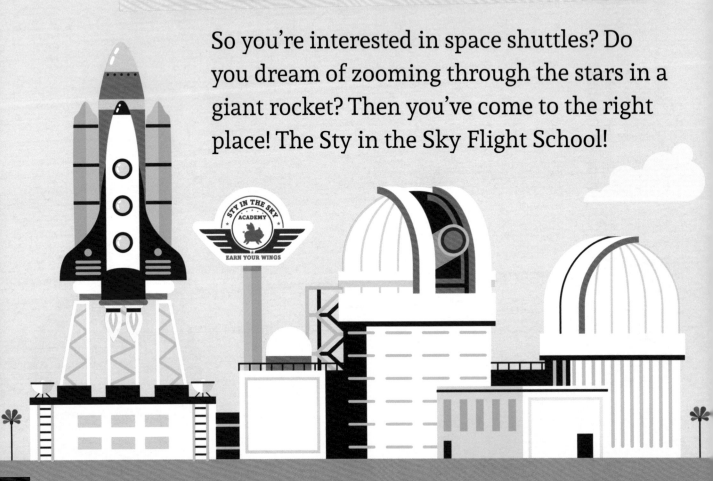

Here, you will learn all you need to know about some amazing spacecraft, and join the **elite** space force known as the Pink Wings! So pay attention: it's time to FLY!

What You Need to Know

How they go UP! ☐

How they come DOWN! ☐

Why so many CONTROLS? ☐

Where is the TOILET? ☐

LESSON 1:
WHAT IS A SPACE SHUTTLE?

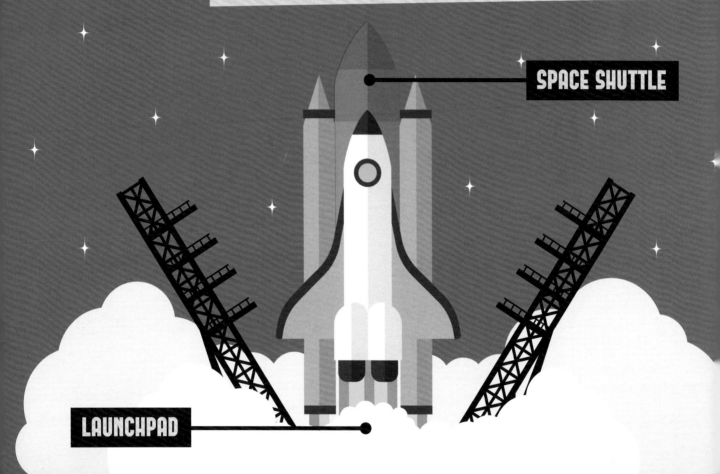

SPACE SHUTTLE

LAUNCHPAD

Space shuttles are a type of spacecraft. This means they can leave Earth's **atmosphere** and explore space.

Shuttles are used to transport important equipment and highly trained __astronauts__.

5...4...3...2...1... TAKEOFF

Space shuttles taking off are VERY LOUD! CAN YOU HEAR ME?!

PIGGLES

7

LESSON 2:

PARTS OF A SPACE SHUTTLE

U.S. SHUTTLES AND RUSSIAN SHUTTLES LOOK DIFFERENT BUT WORK THE SAME WAY.

FUEL TANK

The huge tank on the shuttle holds the fuel the rocket boosters use.

FLIGHT DECK

The crew can operate the orbiter from here.

PAYLOAD BAY

Anything the shuttle carries, like cargo, is called payload, and is stored here.

ENGINES

The engines move and steer the shuttle in space.

Let's look at the parts of a space shuttle.

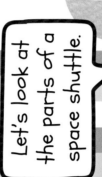

ORBITER

The section that carries the passengers, astronauts, and anything they have brought with them.

ROCKET BOOSTERS

These lift the shuttle off the ground and blast it into space.

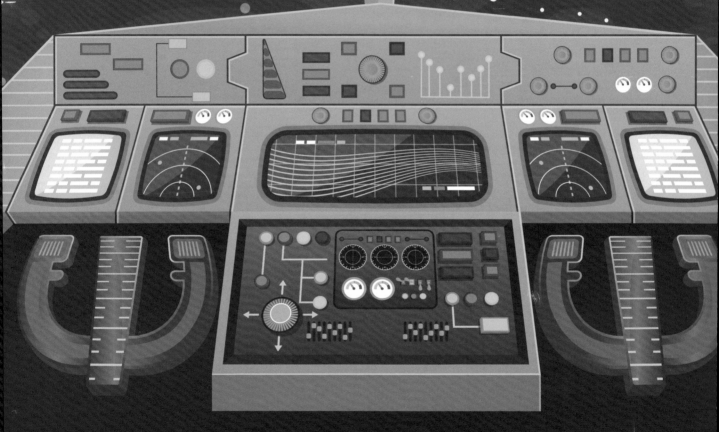

LESSON 3:
INSIDE A SPACE SHUTTLE

The flight deck is where the pilots fly the shuttle. All the controls needed to **maneuver** (say: man-oo-ver) the shuttle are here. There are over 2,020 controls and displays on the flight deck!

The orbiter also holds the living quarters for the crew. Crew sleep, eat, exercise, and even go to the bathroom here. Astronauts have to use special space toilets – it's hard to pee when there is no **gravity**!

THRUST!

To get a shuttle into space, you need thrust. Thrust is a **force** that pushes the shuttle straight up, fast enough to escape Earth's gravity and get into space.

DOWN!

Gas escaping from the fuel tanks very quickly is forced DOWN into the ground.

UP!

This downward force is big enough to push the shuttle UP!

It takes 8 seconds to reach 100 miles (160 km) per hour.

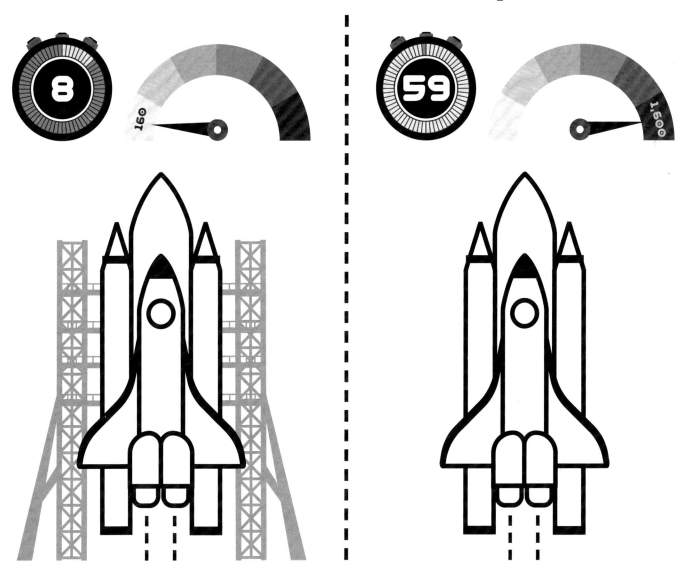

As the fuel is used up, the shuttle gets lighter, and thus faster. After a minute, the shuttle is traveling at about 1,000 miles (1,600 km) per hour!

LESSON 5:
ORBIT!

After launch, the orbiter drops the tanks and boosters into the sea. This makes the shuttle lighter and easier to steer. The shuttle continues into space using its own engines.

The shuttle goes into Low-Earth Orbit (LEO). This means it follows a regular, repeating path, quite close to Earth. It travels at around 16,780 miles (27,000 km) per hour to stay in orbit.

16,780 MPH

It takes about 90 minutes for the orbiter to go around Earth once, so no excuse for being late to class!

PIGGLES

REENTRY AND LANDING

To get back to Earth, the shuttle slows its speed. When it hits the atmosphere, it produces <u>air resistance</u> by flying with its nose up – almost like a belly flop back to Earth!

PIGGLES

The air resistance slows the shuttle down. It gets very hot during reentry!

Once through the atmosphere, the shuttle can behave like a regular airplane, landing on a runway. Computers usually control reentry and the pilot takes over to land the shuttle.

Shuttles land at around 225 mph (360 kph). A parachute helps to slow it down.

PIGGLES

COLUMBIA

On April 12th, 1981, NASA launched their first shuttle at Cape Canaveral. The shuttle, Columbia, was piloted by John Young and Robert Crippen.

VOSTOK 6

In 1963, Valentina Tereshkova became the first woman to fly in space. She piloted the Vostok 6.

HUBBLE TELESCOPE

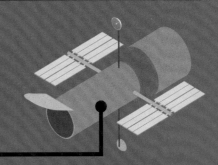

On April 24th, 1990, the shuttle Discovery took the famous Hubble Telescope into orbit.

FIRST ROCKET TO LAND AND BE USED AGAIN

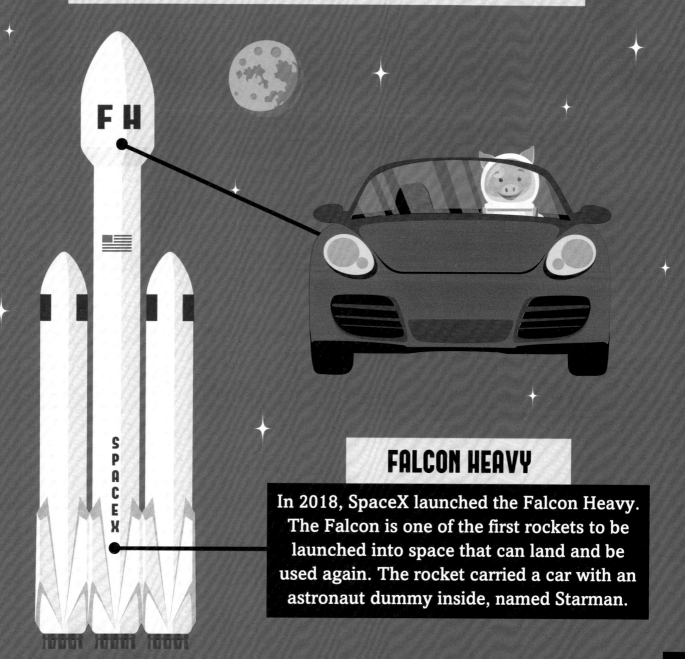

F H

SPACEX

FALCON HEAVY

In 2018, SpaceX launched the Falcon Heavy. The Falcon is one of the first rockets to be launched into space that can land and be used again. The rocket carried a car with an astronaut dummy inside, named Starman.

FLIGHT CHECK

Okay, students. Let's test your knowledge about space shuttles and see if you've been paying attention! Get them all right, and you earn your Pink Wings!

Questions

1. What is cargo on a space shuttle called?

2. What is the name of the force that pushes the rocket upward?

3. What is LEO?

4. At what speed do shuttles land?

5. Who was the first woman to fly in space?

Did you get all the answers right? You did? Well done!

This means you are now an expert astronaut and you have become a member of the world's most elite space force: The Pink Wings!

SPACEWALK!

When in space, sometimes you will need to do repairs or carry out missions. To do this, you will need a special spacesuit to protect you and give you air to breathe...

STEP ONE
Identify Emergency

"SOMEONE BROKE THE SPACE TOILET!"

STEP TWO
Don't Panic

STEP THREE
Attach Rope

GLOSSARY

AIR RESISTANCE when air resists something moving through it

ASTRONAUTS people who are trained to fly in a spacecraft

ATMOSPHERE the mixture of gases that make up the air that surrounds the Earth

ELITE someone or something that is the best of a group

FORCE a power or energy

GRAVITY the force that pulls everything downward toward Earth

MANEUVER steer and control a vehicle

INDEX